STAR TREK™

REDSHIRT'S LITTLE BOOK OF

DOOM

STAR TREK™
REDSHIRT'S LITTLE BOOK OF
DOOM

WRITTEN BY
ROBB PEARLMAN

ILLUSTRATED BY
ANNA-MARIA JUNG

INSIGHT
EDITIONS

San Rafael, California

POOR REDSHIRT.

HE'S *DOOMED.*

HE CAN'T SET FOOT ON A PLANET WITHOUT VIOLATING THE PRIME DIRECTIVE. HE'S INCAPABLE OF LOADING A PHOTON TORPEDO WITHOUT DROPPING IT. AND HE CAN'T EAT A BANANA WITHOUT SERIOUSLY INJURING HIMSELF.

COULD OUR CONSTANT LAUGHING AT HIS FOIBLES SOMEHOW BE WARPING THE SPACE-TIME THAT SURROUNDS HIM INTO A NEXUS OF BAD LUCK AND EMBARRASSMENT?

NAH.

HE'S JUST DOOMED TO SUFFER A NEVER-ENDING SERIES OF MISHAPS AND FAIL AT EVEN THE SMALLEST TASK.

THIS LOOK AT SOME OF REDSHIRT'S MOST ENDEARING CRISES PROVES, ONCE AND FOR ALL, THAT HE'LL NEVER BOLDLY GO ANYWHERE WITHOUT SOME SORT OF CALAMITY BEFALLING HIM.

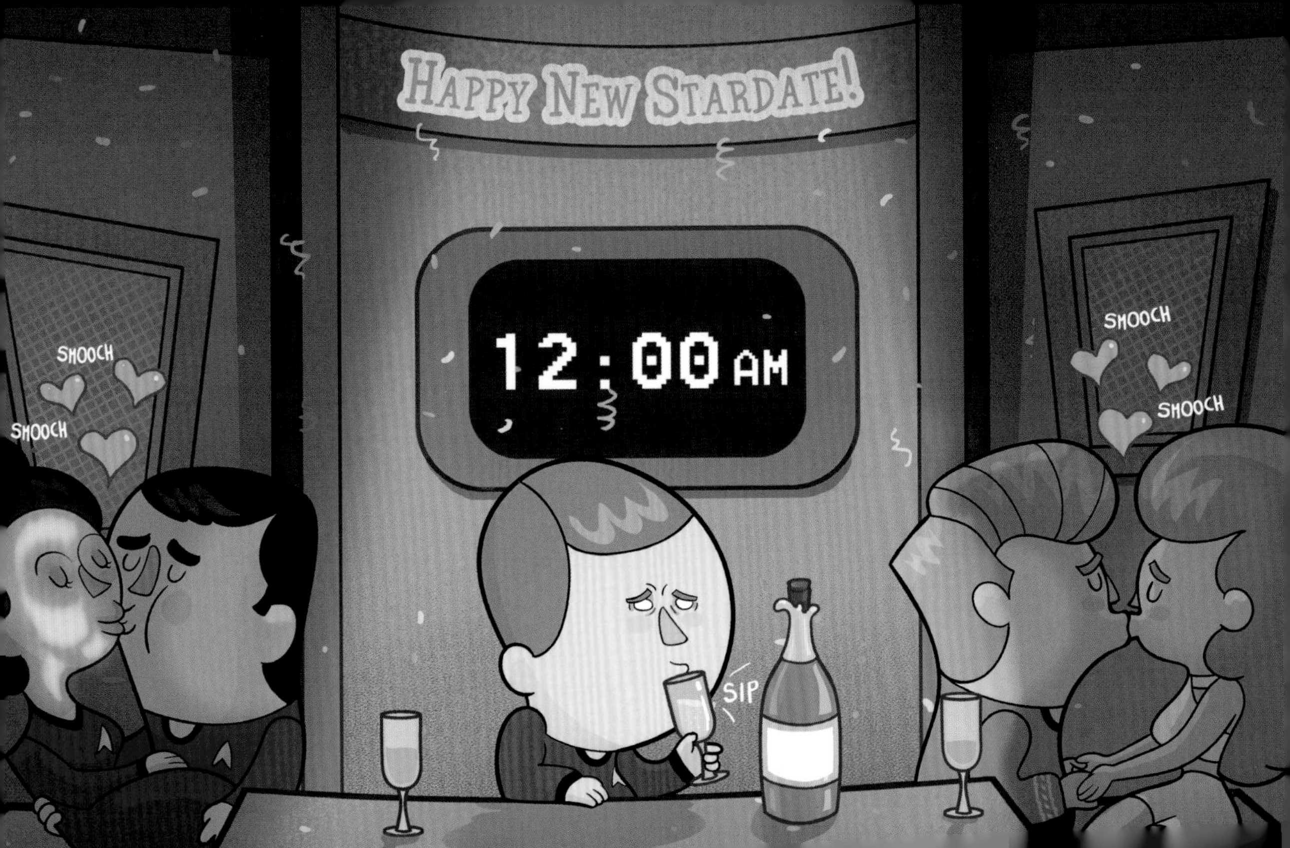
HAPPY NEW STARDATE!
12:00 AM
SMOOCH
SMOOCH
SMOOCH
SMOOCH
SIP

THE **RUNNING** OF THE **HORTAS**

CLOSE CALL!
Man in Red Shirt Saves Edith Keeler's Life!

INSIGHT EDITIONS

PO Box 3088
San Rafael, CA 94912
www.insighteditions.com

Find us on Facebook: www.facebook.com/InsightEditions
Follow us on Twitter: @insighteditions

Published by Insight Editions, San Rafael, California, in
2016. No part of this book may be reproduced in any
form without written permission from the publisher.

Library of Congress Cataloging-in-Publication
Data available.

ISBN: 978-1-60887-736-2

Publisher: Raoul Goff
Acquisitions Manager: Robbie Schmidt
Art Director: Chrissy Kwasnik
Layout: Jenelle Wagner
Executive Editor: Vanessa Lopez
Senior Editor: Chris Prince
Production Editor: Elaine Ou
Production Manager: Blake Mitchum
Editorial Assistant: Katie DeSandro

Insight Editions would like to thank Marian Cordry,
Risa Kessler, and John Van Citters.

ROOTS of PEACE REPLANTED PAPER

Insight Editions, in association with Roots of Peace, will plant
two trees for each tree used in the manufacturing of this book.
Roots of Peace is an internationally renowned humanitarian
organization dedicated to eradicating land mines worldwide and
converting war-torn lands into productive farms and wildlife
habitats. Roots of Peace will plant two million fruit and nut trees
in Afghanistan and provide farmers there with the skills and
support necessary for sustainable land use.

Manufactured in China by Insight Editions

10 9 8 7 6 5 4 3 2 1